# HORRID HENRY

## TRICKS THE TOOTH FAIRY

Francesca Simon

*Illustrated by* Tony Ross

Orion
Children's Books

*For Victor and Susan Bers,*
*and all our good times*

Published in paperback in 1997
First published in Great Britain in 1996
by Orion Children's Books
a division of The Orion Publishing Group Ltd
Orion House
5 Upper St Martin's Lane
London WC2H 9EA

This edition published in 2000

5

A catalogue record for this book
is available from the British Library

Typeset by Deltatype Ltd, Birkenhead
Printed in Great Britain by Clays Ltd, St Ives plc

www.orionbooks.co.uk

# CONTENTS

# 1

# HORRID HENRY TRICKS THE TOOTH FAIRY

"It's not fair!" shrieked Horrid Henry. He trampled on Dad's new flower-bed, squashing the pansies. "It's just not fair!"

Moody Margaret had lost two teeth. Sour Susan had lost three. Clever Clare lost two in one day. Rude Ralph had lost four, two top and two bottom, and could spit to the blackboard from his desk. Greedy Graham's teeth were pouring out. Even Weepy William had lost one – and that was ages ago.

Every day someone swaggered into school showing off a big black toothy gap and waving fifty pence or even a pound that the Tooth Fairy had brought. Everyone, that is, but Henry.

"It's not fair!" shouted Henry again. He yanked on his teeth. He pulled, he pushed, he tweaked, and he tugged.

They would not budge.

His teeth were superglued to his gums.

"Why me?" moaned Henry, stomping on the petunias. "Why am I the only one who hasn't lost a tooth?"

Horrid Henry sat in his fort and scowled. He was sick and tired of other kids flaunting their ugly wobbly teeth and disgusting holes in their gums. The next person who so much as mentioned the word "tooth" had better watch out.

"HENRY!" shouted a squeaky little voice. "Where are you?"

Horrid Henry hid behind the branches.

"I know you're in the fort, Henry," said Perfect Peter.

"Go away!" said Henry.

"Look, Henry," said Peter. "I've got something wonderful to show you."

Henry scowled. "What?"

"You have to see it," said Peter.

Peter never had anything good to show. His idea of something wonderful was a new stamp, or a book about plants, or a gold star from his teacher saying how perfect he'd been. Still . . .

Henry crawled out.

"This had better be good," he said. "Or you're in big trouble."

Peter held out his fist and opened it.

There was something small and white in Peter's hand. It looked like . . . no, it couldn't be.

Henry stared at Peter. Peter smiled as

9

wide as he could. Henry's jaw dropped.
This was impossible. His eyes must be
playing tricks on him.

Henry blinked. Then he blinked again.

His eyes were not playing tricks.
Perfect Peter, his *younger* brother, had a
black gap at the bottom of his mouth
where a tooth had been.

Henry grabbed Peter. "You've
coloured in your tooth with black crayon,
you faker."

"Have not!" shrieked Peter. "It fell
out. See."

Peter proudly poked his finger through
the hole in his mouth.

It was true. Perfect Peter had lost a tooth. Henry felt as if a fist had slammed into his stomach.

"Told you," said Peter. He smiled again at Henry.

Henry could not bear to look at Peter's gappy teeth a second longer. This was the worst thing that had ever happened to him.

"I hate you!" shrieked Henry. He was a volcano pouring hot molten lava on to the puny human foolish enough to get in his way.

"AAAAGGGGHHHH!" screeched Peter, dropping the tooth.

Henry grabbed it.

"OWWWW!" yelped Peter. "Give me back my tooth!"

"Stop being horrid, Henry!" shouted Mum.

Henry dangled the tooth in front of Peter.

"Nah nah ne nah nah," jeered Henry.

Peter burst into tears.

"Give me back my tooth!" screamed Peter.

Mum ran into the garden.

"Give Peter his tooth this minute," said Mum.

"No," said Henry.

Mum looked fierce. She put out her hand. "Give it to me right now."

Henry dropped the tooth on the ground.

"There," said Horrid Henry.

"That's it, Henry," said Mum. "No pudding tonight."

Henry was too miserable to care.

Peter scooped up his tooth. "Look, Mum," said Peter.

"My big boy!" said Mum, giving him a hug. "How wonderful."

"I'm going to use my money from the Tooth Fairy to buy some stamps for my collection," said Peter.

"What a good idea," said Mum.

Henry stuck out his tongue.

"Henry's sticking out his tongue at me," said Peter.

"Stop it, Henry," said Mum. "Peter, keep that tooth safe for the Tooth Fairy."

"I will," said Peter. He closed his fist tightly round the tooth.

13

Henry sat in his fort. If a tooth wouldn't fall out, he would have to help it. But what to do? He could take a hammer and smash one out. Or he could tie string round a tooth, tie the string round a door handle and slam the door. Eek! Henry grabbed his jaw.

On second thoughts, perhaps not. Maybe there was a less painful way of losing a tooth. What was it the dentist always said? Eat too many sweets and your teeth will fall out?

Horrid Henry sneaked into the kitchen. He looked to the right. He looked to the left. No one was there. From the sitting room came the screechy scratchy sound of Peter practising his cello.

Henry dashed to the cupboard where Mum kept the sweet jar. Sweet day was Saturday, and today was Thursday. Two whole days before he got into trouble.

Henry stuffed as many sticky sweets into his mouth as fast as he could.

Chomp Chomp Chomp Chomp.

Chomp Chew Chomp Chew.

Chompa Chew Chompa Chew.

Chompa . . . Chompa . . .

Chompa . . .

Chompa . . .

Chew.

Henry's jaw started to slow down. He put the last sticky toffee in his mouth and forced his teeth to move up and down.

Henry started to feel sick. His teeth felt even sicker. He wiggled them hopefully. After all that sugar one was sure to fall out. He could see all the comics he would buy with his pound already.

Henry wiggled his teeth again. And again.

Nothing moved.

Rats, thought Henry. His mouth hurt. His gums hurt. His tummy hurt. What did a boy have to do to get a tooth?

Then Henry had a wonderful, spectacular idea. It was so wonderful that he hugged himself. Why should Peter get a pound from the Tooth Fairy? Henry would get that pound, not him. And how? Simple. He would trick the Tooth Fairy.

The house was quiet. Henry tip-toed into Peter's room. There was Peter, sound asleep, a big smile on his face. Henry sneaked his hand under Peter's pillow and stole the tooth.

Tee hee, thought Henry. He tiptoed out of Peter's room and bumped into Mum.

"AAAAGGGHH!" shrieked Henry.

"AAAAGGGHH!" shrieked Mum.

"You scared me," said Henry.

"What are you doing?" said Mum.

"Nothing," said Henry. "I thought I heard a noise in Peter's room and went to check."

Mum looked at Henry. Henry tried to look sweet.

"Go back to bed, Henry," said Mum.

Henry scampered to his room and put the tooth under his pillow. Phew. That was a close call. Henry smiled. Wouldn't

that cry-baby Peter be furious the next
morning when he found no tooth and no
money?

Henry woke up and felt under his pillow.
The tooth was gone. Hurray, thought
Henry. Now for the money.

Henry searched under the pillow.

Henry searched on top of the pillow. He searched under the covers, under Teddy, under the bed, everywhere. There was no money.

Henry heard Peter's footsteps pounding down the hall.

"Mum, Dad, look," said Peter. "A whole pound from the Tooth Fairy!"

"Great!" said Mum.

19

"Wonderful!" said Dad.

What?! thought Henry.

"Shall I share it with you, Mum?" said Peter.

"Thank you, darling Peter, but no thanks," said Mum. "It's for you."

"I'll have it," said Henry. "There are loads of comics I want to buy. And some –"

"No," said Peter. "It's mine. Get your own tooth."

Henry stared at his brother. Peter would never have dared to speak to him like that before.

Horrid Henry pretended he was a pirate captain pushing a prisoner off the plank.

"OWWW!" shrieked Peter.

"Don't be horrid, Henry," said Dad.

Henry decided to change the subject fast.

"Mum," said Henry. "How does the Tooth Fairy *know* who's lost a tooth?"

"She looks under the pillow," said Mum.

"But how does she know whose pillow to look under?"

"She just does," said Mum. "By magic."

"But how?" said Henry.

"She sees the gap between your teeth," said Mum.

Aha, thought Henry. That's where he'd gone wrong.

That night Henry cut out a small piece of black paper, wet it, and covered over his two bottom teeth. He smiled at himself in the mirror. Perfect, thought Henry. He smiled again.

Then Henry stuck a pair of dracula

21

teeth under his pillow. He tied a string round the biggest tooth, and tied the string to his finger. When the Tooth Fairy came, the string would pull on his finger and wake him up.

All right, Tooth Fairy, thought Henry. You think you're so smart. Find your way out of this one.

The next morning was Saturday. Henry woke up and felt under his pillow. The string was still attached to his finger, but the dracula teeth were gone. In their place was something small and round . . .

"My pound coin!" crowed Henry. He grabbed it.

The pound coin was plastic.

There must be some mistake, thought Henry. He checked under the pillow again. But all he found was a folded piece of bright blue paper, covered in stars.

Henry opened it. There, in tiny gold letters, he read:

"Rats," said Henry.

From downstairs came the sound of Mum shouting.

"Henry! Get down here this minute!"

"What now?" muttered Henry, heaving his heavy bones out of bed.

"Yeah?" said Henry.

Mum held up an empty jar.

"Well?" said Mum.

Henry had forgotten all about the sweets.

"It wasn't me," said Henry automatically. "We must have mice."

"No sweets for a month," said Mum. "You'll eat apples instead. You can start right now."

Ugh. Apples. Henry hated all fruits and vegetables, but apples were the worst.

"Oh no," said Henry.

"Oh yes," said Mum. "Right now."

Henry took the apple and bit off the teeniest, tiniest piece he could.

CRUNCH. CRACK.

Henry choked. Then he swallowed, gasping and spluttering.

His mouth felt funny. Henry poked around with his tongue and felt a space.

He shoved his fingers in his mouth,
then ran to the mirror.

His tooth was gone.

He'd swallowed it.

"It's not fair!" shrieked Horrid Henry.

# 2

............................................

# HORRID HENRY'S WEDDING

"I'm not wearing these horrible clothes and that's that!"

Horrid Henry glared at the mirror. A stranger smothered in a lilac ruffled shirt, green satin knickerbockers, tights, pink cummerbund tied in a floppy bow and pointy white satin shoes with gold buckles glared back at him.

Henry had never seen anyone looking so silly in his life.

"Aha ha ha ha ha!" shrieked Horrid Henry, pointing at the mirror.

Then Henry peered more closely. The ridiculous looking boy was him.

Perfect Peter stood next to Horrid Henry. He too was smothered in a lilac ruffled shirt, green satin knickerbockers, tights, pink cummerbund and pointy white shoes with gold buckles. But, unlike Henry, Peter was smiling.

"Aren't they adorable!" squealed Prissy Polly. "That's how my children are always going to dress."

Prissy Polly was Horrid Henry's horrible older cousin. Prissy Polly was always squeaking and squealing:

"Eeek, it's a speck of dust."

"Eeek, it's a puddle."

"Eeek, my hair is a mess."

But when Prissy Polly announced she was getting married to Pimply Paul and wanted Henry and Peter to be pageboys, Mum said yes before Henry could stop her.

"What's a pageboy?" asked Henry suspiciously.

"A pageboy carries the wedding rings down the aisle on a satin cushion," said Mum.

"And throws confetti afterwards," said Dad.

Henry liked the idea of throwing confetti. But carrying rings on a cushion? No thanks.

"I don't want to be a pageboy," said Henry.

"I do, I do," said Peter.

"You're going to be a pageboy, and that's that," said Mum.

"And you'll behave yourself," said Dad. "It's very kind of cousin Polly to ask you."

Henry scowled.

"Who'd want to be married to *her*?" said Henry. "I wouldn't if you paid me a million pounds."

But for some reason the bridegroom, Pimply Paul, did want to marry Prissy Polly. And, as far as Henry knew, he had not been paid one million pounds.

Pimply Paul was also trying on his wedding clothes. He looked ridiculous in a black top hat, lilac shirt, and a black jacket covered in gold swirls.

"I won't wear these silly clothes," said Henry.

"Oh be quiet, you little brat," snapped Pimply Paul.

Horrid Henry glared at him.

"I won't," said Henry. "And that's final."

"Henry, stop being horrid," said Mum. She looked extremely silly in a big floppy hat dripping with flowers.

Suddenly Henry grabbed at the lace ruffles round his throat.

30

"I'm choking," he gasped. "I can't breathe."

Then Henry fell to the floor and rolled around.

"Uggggghhhhhhh," moaned Henry. "I'm dying."

"Get up this minute, Henry!" said Dad.

"Eeek, there's dirt on the floor!" shrieked Polly.

"Can't you control that child?" hissed Pimply Paul.

"I DON'T WANT TO BE A PAGEBOY!" howled Horrid Henry.

"Thank you so much for asking me to be a pageboy, Polly," shouted Perfect Peter, trying to be heard over Henry's screams.

"You're welcome," shouted Polly.

"Stop that, Henry!" ordered Mum. "I've never been so ashamed in my life."

"I hate children," muttered Pimply Paul under his breath.

Horrid Henry stopped. Unfortunately, his pageboy clothes looked as fresh and crisp as ever.

All right, thought Horrid Henry. You want me at this wedding? You've got me.

Prissy Polly's wedding day arrived. Henry

was delighted to see rain pouring down.
How cross Polly would be.

Perfect Peter was already dressed.

"Isn't this going to be fun, Henry?"
said Peter.

"No!" said Henry, sitting on the floor.
"And I'm not going."

Mum and Dad stuffed Henry into his
pageboy clothes. It was hard, heavy work.

Finally everyone was in the car.

"We're going to be late!" shrieked
Mum.

"We're going to be late!" shrieked
Dad.

"We're going to be late!" shrieked
Peter.

"Good!" muttered Henry.

Mum, Dad, Henry and Peter arrived at
the church. Boom! There was a clap of
thunder. Rain poured down. All the
other guests were already inside.

"Watch out for the puddle, boys," said Mum, as she leapt out of the car. She opened her umbrella.

Dad jumped over the puddle.

Peter jumped over the puddle.

Henry jumped over the puddle, and tripped.

SPLASH!

"Oopsy," said Henry.

His ruffles were torn, his knickerbockers were filthy, and his satin shoes were soaked.

Mum, Dad, and Peter were covered in muddy water.

Perfect Peter burst into tears.

"You've ruined my pageboy clothes," sobbed Peter.

Mum wiped as much dirt as she could off Henry and Peter.

"It was an accident, Mum, really," said Henry.

"Hurry up, you're late!" shouted Pimply Paul.

Mum and Dad dashed into the church. Henry and Peter stayed outside, waiting to make their entrance.

Pimply Paul and his best man, Cross Colin, stared at Henry and Peter.

"You look a mess," said Paul.

"It was an accident," said Henry.

Peter snivelled.

"Now be careful with the wedding rings," said Cross Colin. He handed

Henry and Peter a satin cushion each, with a gold ring on top.

A great quivering clump of lace and taffeta and bows and flowers approached. Henry guessed Prissy Polly must be lurking somewhere underneath.

"Eeek," squeaked the clump. "Why did it have to rain on my wedding?"

"Eeek," squeaked the clump again. "You're filthy."

Perfect Peter began to sob. The satin cushion trembled in his hand. The ring balanced precariously near the edge.

Cross Colin snatched Peter's cushion.

"You can't carry a ring with your hand shaking like that," snapped Colin. "You'd better carry them both, Henry."

"Come *on*," hissed Pimply Paul. "We're late!"

Cross Colin and Pimply Paul dashed into the church.

The music started. Henry pranced down the aisle after Polly. Everyone stood up.

Henry beamed and bowed and waved. He was King Henry the Horrible, smiling graciously at his cheering subjects before he chopped off their heads.

As he danced along, he stepped on Polly's long, trailing dress.

Riiiiip.

"Eeeeek!" squeaked Prissy Polly.

Part of Polly's train lay beneath Henry's muddy satin shoe.

That dress was too long anyway, thought Henry. He kicked the fabric out of the way and stomped down the aisle.

The bride, groom, best man, and pageboys assembled in front of the minister.

Henry stood . . . and stood . . . and stood. The minister droned on . . . and

on . . . and on. Henry's arm holding up
the cushion began to ache.

This is boring, thought Henry, jiggling
the rings on the cushion.

Boing! Boing! Boing!

Oooh, thought Henry. I'm good at
ring tossing.

The rings bounced.

The minister droned.

Henry was a famous pancake chef,
tossing the pancakes higher and higher
and higher . . .

Clink clunk.

The rings rolled down the aisle and
vanished down a small grate.

Oops, thought Henry.

"May I have the rings, please?" said the
minister.

Everyone looked at Henry.

"He's got them," said Henry
desperately, pointing at Peter.

"I have not," sobbed Peter.

Henry reached into his pocket. He found two pieces of old chewing-gum, some gravel, and his lucky pirate ring.

"Here, use this," he said.

At last, Pimply Paul and Prissy Polly were married.

Cross Colin handed Henry and Peter a basket of pink and yellow rose petals each.

"Throw the petals in front of the bride and groom as they walk back down the aisle," whispered Colin.

"I will," said Peter. He scattered the petals before Pimply Paul and Prissy Polly.

"So will I," said Henry. He hurled a handful of petals in Pimply Paul's face.

"Watch it, you little brat," snarled Paul.

"Windy, isn't it?" said Henry. He hurled another handful of petals at Polly.

"Eeek," squeaked Prissy Polly.

"Everyone outside for the photographs," said the photographer.

Horrid Henry loved having his picture

taken. He dashed out.

"Pictures of the bride and groom first," said the photographer.

Henry jumped in front.

Click.

Henry peeked from the side.

Click.

Henry stuck out his tongue.
Click.
Henry made horrible rude faces.
Click.

"This way to the reception!" said
Cross Colin.

The wedding party was held in a nearby hotel.

The adults did nothing but talk and eat, talk and drink, talk and eat.

Perfect Peter sat at the table and ate his lunch.

Horrid Henry sat under the table and poked people's legs. He crawled around and squashed some toes. Then Henry got bored and drifted into the next room.

There was the wedding cake, standing alone, on a little table. It was the most beautiful, delicious-looking cake Henry had ever seen. It had three layers and was covered in luscious white icing and yummy iced flowers and bells and leaves.

Henry's mouth watered.

I'll just taste a teeny weeny bit of petal, thought Henry. No harm in that.

He broke off a morsel and popped it in his mouth.

Hmmmm boy! That icing tasted great.

Perhaps just one more bite, thought Henry. If I take it from the back, no one will notice.

Henry carefully selected an icing rose from the bottom tier and stuffed it in his mouth. Wow.

Henry stood back from the cake. It looked a little uneven now, with that rose missing from the bottom.

I'll just even it up, thought Henry. It was the work of a moment to break off a rose from the middle tier and another from the top.

Then a strange thing happened.

"Eat me," whispered the cake. "Go on."

Who was Henry to ignore such a request?

He picked out a few crumbs from the back.

44

Delicious, thought Henry. Then he took a few more. And a few more. Then he dug out a nice big chunk.

"What do you think you're doing?" shouted Pimply Paul.

Henry ran round the cake table. Paul ran after him.

Round and round and round the cake they ran.

"Just wait till I get my hands on you!" snarled Pimply Paul.

45

Henry dashed under the table.

Pimply Paul lunged for him and missed.

SPLAT.

Pimply Paul fell head first on to the cake.

Henry slipped away.

Prissy Polly ran into the room.

"Eeek," she shrieked.


"Wasn't that a lovely wedding," sighed Mum on the way home. "Funny they didn't have a cake, though."

"Oh yes," said Dad.

"Oh yes," said Peter.

"OH YES!" said Henry. "I'll be glad to be a pageboy anytime."

# 3

## MOODY MARGARET MOVES IN

Mum was on the phone.

"Of course we'd be delighted to have Margaret," she said. "It will be no trouble at all."

Henry stopped breaking the tails off Peter's plastic horses.

"WHAT?" he howled.

"Shh, Henry," said Mum. "No, no," she added. "Henry is delighted, too. See you Friday."

"What's going on?" said Henry.

"Margaret is coming to stay while her

parents go on holiday," said Mum.

Henry was speechless with horror.

"She's going to stay . . . here?"

"Yes," said Mum.

"How long?" said Henry.

"Two weeks," said Mum brightly.

Horrid Henry could not stand Moody Margaret for more than two minutes.

"Two weeks?" he said. "I'll run away! I'll lock her out of the house, I'll pull her hair out, I'll . . ."

"Don't be horrid, Henry," said Mum. "Margaret's a lovely girl and I'm sure we'll have fun."

"No we won't," said Henry. "Not with that moody old grouch."

"I'll have fun," said Perfect Peter. "I love having guests."

"She's not sleeping in my room," said Horrid Henry. "She can sleep in the cellar."

"No," said Mum. "You'll move into Peter's room and let Margaret have your bed."

Horrid Henry opened his mouth to scream, but only a rasping sound came out. He was so appalled he could only gasp.

"Give . . . up . . . my . . . room!" he choked. "To . . . Margaret?"

Margaret spying on *his* treasures, sleeping in *his* bed, playing with *his* toys while he had to share a room with Peter . . .

"No!" howled Henry. He fell on the floor and screamed. "NO!!"

"I don't mind giving up my bed for a guest," said Perfect Peter. "It's the polite thing to do. Guests come first."

Henry stopped howling just long enough to kick Peter.

"Owww!" screamed Peter. He burst

into tears, "Mum!"

"Henry!" yelled Mum. "You horrid boy! Say sorry to Peter."

"She's not coming!" shrieked Henry. "And that's final."

"Go to your room!" yelled Mum.

Moody Margaret arrived at Henry's house with her parents, four suitcases, seven boxes of toys, two pillows, and a trumpet.

"Margaret won't be any trouble," said her mum. "She's always polite, eats everything, and never complains. Isn't that right, Precious?"

"Yes," said Margaret.

"Margaret's no fusspot," said her dad. "She's good as gold, aren't you, Precious?"

"Yes," said Margaret.

"Have a lovely holiday," said Mum.

"We will," said Margaret's parents.

The door slammed behind them.

Moody Margaret marched into the sitting room and swept a finger across the mantelpiece.

"It's not very clean, is it?" she said. "You'd never find so much dust at *my* house."

"Oh," said Dad.

"A little dust never hurt anyone," said Mum.

"I'm allergic," said Margaret. "One whiff of dust and I start to . . . sn . . . sn . . . ACHOOO!" she sneezed.

"We'll clean up right away," said Mum.

Dad mopped.

Mum swept.

Peter dusted.

Henry hoovered.

Margaret directed.

"Henry, you've missed a big dust-ball right there," said Margaret, pointing under the sofa.

Horrid Henry hoovered as far away from the dust as possible.

"Not there, here!" said Margaret.

Henry aimed the hoover at Margaret. He was a fire-breathing dragon burning his prey to a crisp.

"Help!" shrieked Margaret.

"Henry!" said Dad.

"Don't be horrid," said Mum.

"I think Henry should be punished," said Margaret. "I think he should be locked in his bedroom for three weeks."

"I don't have a bedroom to be locked up in 'cause you're in it," said Henry. He glared at Margaret.

Margaret glared back.

"I'm the guest, Henry, so you'd better be polite," hissed Margaret.

"Of course he'll be polite," said Mum. "Don't worry, Margaret. Any trouble, you come straight to me."

"Thank you," said Moody Margaret, smiling. "I will. I'm hungry," she added. "Why isn't supper ready?"

"It will be soon," said Dad.

"But I *always* eat at six o'clock," said Margaret, "I want to eat NOW."

"All right," said Dad.

Horrid Henry and Moody Margaret dashed for the seat facing the garden. Margaret got there first. Henry shoved her off. Then Margaret shoved him off.

Thud. Henry landed on the floor.

"Ouch," said Henry.

"Let the guest have the chair," said Dad.

"But that's *my* chair," said Henry. "That's where I *always* sit."

"Have my chair, Margaret," said Perfect Peter. "I don't mind."

"I want to sit here," said Moody Margaret. "I'm the guest so *I* decide."

Horrid Henry dragged himself around the table and sat next to Peter.

"OUCH!" shrieked Margaret. "Henry kicked me!"

"No I didn't," said Henry, outraged.

"Stop it, Henry," said Mum. "That's no way to treat a guest."

Henry stuck out his tongue at
Margaret. Moody Margaret stuck out her
tongue even further, then stomped on his
foot.

"OUCH!" shrieked Henry. "Margaret
kicked me!"

Moody Margaret gasped. "Oh I'm ever

so sorry, Henry," she said sweetly. "It was an accident. Silly me. I didn't mean to, really I didn't."

Dad brought the food to the table.

"What's *that*?" asked Margaret.

"Baked beans, corn on the cob, and chicken," said Dad.

"I don't like baked beans," said Margaret. "And I like my corn *off* the cob."

Mum scraped the corn off the cob.

"No, put the corn on a separate plate!" shrieked Margaret. "I don't like vegetables touching my meat."

Dad got out the pirate plate, the duck plate, and the "Happy birthday Peter" plate.

"I want the pirate plate," said Margaret, snatching it.

"I want the pirate plate," said Henry, snatching it back.

"I don't mind which plate I get," said Perfect Peter. "A plate's a plate."

"No it isn't!" shouted Henry.

"I'm the guest," shouted Margaret. "I get to choose."

"Give her the pirate plate, Henry," said Dad.

"It's not fair," said Henry, glaring at his plate decorated with little ducks.

"She's the guest," said Mum.

"So?" said Henry. Wasn't there an ancient Greek who stretched all his guests on an iron bed if they were too short or lopped off their heads and feet if they were too long? That guy sure knew how to deal with horrible guests like Moody Margaret.

"Yuck," said Margaret, spitting out a mouthful of chicken. "You've put salt on it!"

"Only a little," said Dad.

58

"I never eat salt," said Moody Margaret. "It's not good for me. And I always have peas at *my* house."

"We'll get some tomorrow," said Mum.

Peter lay asleep in the top bunk. Horrid Henry sat listening by the door. He'd scattered crumbs all over Margaret's bed. He couldn't wait to hear her scream.

But there wasn't a sound coming from Henry's room, where Margaret the invader lay. Henry couldn't understand it.

Sadly, he climbed into (oh, the shame of it) the *bottom* bunk. Then he screamed. His bed was filled with jam, crumbs, and something squishy squashy and horrible.

"Go to sleep, Henry!" shouted Dad.

That Margaret! He'd booby-trap the room, cut up her doll's clothes, paint her face purple . . . Henry smiled grimly. Oh yes, he'd fix Moody Margaret.

Mum and Dad sat in the sitting room watching TV.

Moody Margaret appeared on the stairs.

"I can't sleep with that noise," she said.

Mum and Dad looked at each other.

"We are watching very quietly, dear," said Mum.

"But I can't sleep if there's any noise in the house," said Margaret. "I have very sensitive ears."

Mum turned off the TV and picked up her knitting needles.

Click click click.

Margaret reappeared.

"I can't sleep with that clicking noise," she said.

"All right," said Mum. She sighed a little.

"And it's cold in my bedroom," said Moody Margaret.

Mum turned up the heat.

Margaret reappeared.

"Now it's too hot," said Moody Margaret.

Dad turned down the heat.

"My room smells funny," said Margaret.

"My bed is too hard," said Margaret.

"My room is too stuffy," said Margaret.

"My room is too light," said Margaret.

"Goodnight, Margaret," said Mum.

"How many more days is she staying?" said Dad.

Mum looked at the calendar.

"Only thirteen," said Mum.

Dad hid his face in his hands.

"I don't know if I can live that long," said Dad.


TOOTA TOOT. Mum blasted out of bed.

TOOTA TOOT. Dad blasted out of bed.

TOOTA TOOT. TOOTA TOOT.

TOOTA TOOT TOOT TOOT. Henry and Peter blasted out of bed.

Margaret marched down the hall, playing her trumpet.

TOOTA TOOT. TOOTA TOOT.

TOOTA TOOT TOOT TOOT
TOOT.

"Margaret, would you mind playing your trumpet a little later?" said Dad, clutching his ears. "It's six o'clock in the morning."

"That's when I wake up," said Margaret.

"Could you play a little more softly?" said Mum.

"But I have to practise," said Moody Margaret.

The trumpet blared through the house. TOOT TOOT TOOT.

Horrid Henry turned on his boom box.

BOOM BOOM BOOM.

Margaret played her trumpet louder. TOOT! TOOT! TOOT!

Henry blasted his boom box as loud as he could.

BOOM! BOOM! BOOM!

"Henry!" shrieked Mum.

"Turn that down!" bellowed Dad.

"Quiet!" screamed Margaret. "I can't practise with all this noise." She put down her trumpet. "And I'm hungry. Where's my breakfast?"

"We have breakfast at eight," said Mum.

"But I want breakfast now," said Margaret.

Mum had had enough.

"No," said Mum firmly. "We eat at eight."

Margaret opened her mouth and screamed. No one could scream as long, or as loud, as Moody Margaret.

Her piercing screams echoed through the house.

"All right," said Mum. She knew when she was beaten. "We'll eat now."

Henry's diary.

Monday *I put crumbs in Margaret's bed. She put jam, crusts and slugs in mine.*

Tuesday *Margaret found my secret biscuits and crisps and ate every single one.*

Wednesday *I can't play tapes at night because it disturbs grumpy-face Margaret.*

Thursday *I can't sing because it disturbs frog-face.*

Friday *I can't breathe because it disturbs misery-guts.*

Saturday

*I can stand it No Longer*

That night, when everyone was asleep, Horrid Henry crept into the sitting room and picked up the phone.

"I'd like to leave a message," he whispered.

Bang bang bang bang bang.

Ding dong! Ding dong! Ding dong!

Henry sat up in bed.

Someone was banging on the front door and ringing the bell.

"Who could that be at this time of night?" yawned Mum.

Dad peeked through the window then opened the door.

"Where's my baby?" shouted Margaret's mum.

"Where's my baby?" shouted Margaret's dad.

"Upstairs," said Mum. "Where else?"

"What's happened to her?" shrieked Margaret's mum.

"We got here as quick as we could!" shrieked Margaret's dad.

Mum and Dad looked at each other. What was going on?

"She's fine," said Mum.

Margaret's mum and dad looked at each other. What was going on?

"But the message said it was an emergency and to come at once," said Margaret's mum.

"We cut short our holiday," said Margaret's dad.

"What message?" said Mum.

"What's going on? I can't sleep with all this noise," said Moody Margaret.

Margaret and her parents had gone home.

"What a terrible mix-up," said Mum.

"Such a shame they cut short their holiday," said Dad.

'Still . . ." said Mum. She looked at Dad.

"Hmmn," said Dad.

"You don't think that Henry . . ." said Mum.

"Not even Henry could do something so horrid," said Dad.

Mum frowned.

"Henry!" said Mum.

Henry continued sticking Peter's stamps together.

"Yeah?"

"Do you know anything about a message?"

"Me?" said Henry.

"You," said Mum.

"No," said Henry. "It's a mystery."

"That's a lie, Henry," said Perfect Peter.

"Is not," said Henry.

"Is too," said Peter. "I heard you on the phone."

Henry lunged at Peter. He was a mad bull charging the matador.

"YOWWWWW," shrieked Peter.

Henry stopped. He was in for it now. No pocket money for a year. No sweets for ten years. No TV ever.

Henry squared his shoulders and waited for his punishment.

Dad put his feet up.

"That was a terrible thing to do," said Dad.

Mum turned on the TV.

"Go to your room," said Mum.

Henry bounced upstairs. Your room. Sweeter words were never spoken.

# 4

# HORRID HENRY'S NEW TEACHER

"Now Henry," said Dad. "Today is the first day of school. A chance for a fresh start with a new teacher."

"Yeah, yeah," scowled Horrid Henry.

He hated the first day of term. Another year, another teacher to show who was boss. His first teacher, Miss Marvel, had run screaming from the classroom after two weeks. His next teacher, Mrs Zip, had run screaming from the classroom after one day. Breaking in new teachers wasn't easy, thought Henry, but someone had to do it.

Dad got out a piece of paper and waved it.

"Henry, I never want to read another school report like this again," he said. "Why can't your school reports be like Peter's?"

Henry started whistling.

"Pay attention, Henry," shouted Dad. "This is important. Look at this report."

HENRY'S SCHOOL REPORT

It has been horrible Teaching Henry this year. He is rude, lazy and disruptive. The worst student I have ever taught.

Behaviour: Horrid

English: Horrid

Maths: Horrid

Science: Horrid

P.E: Horrid

"What about *my* report?" said Perfect Peter.

Dad beamed.

"Your report was perfect, Peter," said Dad. "Keep up the wonderful work."

PETER'S SCHOOL REPORT

It has been a pleasure teaching Peter this year. He is polite, hard-working and co-operative. The best student I have ever taught.

Behaviour: Perfect

English: Perfect

Maths: Perfect

Science: Perfect

P.E: Perfect

Peter smiled proudly.

"You'll just have to try harder, Henry," said Peter, smirking.

Horrid Henry was a shark sinking his teeth into a drowning sailor.

"OWWWW," shrieked Peter. "Henry bit me!"

"Don't be horrid, Henry!" shouted Dad. "Or no TV for a week."

"I don't care," muttered Henry. When he became King he'd make it a law that parents, not children, had to go to school.

Horrid Henry pushed and shoved his way into class and grabbed the seat next to Rude Ralph.

"Nah nah ne nah nah, I've got a new football," said Ralph.

Henry didn't have a football. He'd kicked his through Moody Margaret's window.

"Who cares?" said Horrid Henry.

The classroom door slammed. It was

Mr Nerdon, the toughest, meanest, nastiest teacher in the school.

"SILENCE!" he said, glaring at them with his bulging eyes. "I don't want to hear a sound. I don't even want to hear anyone breathe."

The class held its breath.

"GOOD!" he growled. "I'm Mr Nerdon."

Henry snorted. What a stupid name.

"Nerd," he whispered to Ralph.

Rude Ralph giggled.

"Nerdy Nerd," whispered Horrid Henry, snickering.

Mr Nerdon walked up to Henry and jabbed his finger in his face.

"Quiet, you horrible boy!" said Mr Nerdon. "I've got my eye on you. Oh yes. I've heard about your other teachers. Bah! I'm made of stronger stuff. There will be no nonsense in *my* class."

We'll see about that, thought Henry.

"Our first sums for the year are on the board. Now get to work," ordered Mr Nerdon.

Horrid Henry had an idea.

Quickly he scribbled a note to Ralph.

Ralph – I bet you that I can make Mr. Nerdon run screaming out of class by the end of lunchtime.

No way, Henry

If I do will you give me your new football?

O.K. But if you don't, you have to give me your pound coin.

O.K.

Horrid Henry took a deep breath and went to work. He rolled up some paper, stuffed it in his mouth, and spat it out. The spitball whizzed through the air and pinged Mr Nerdon on the back of his neck.

Mr Nerdon wheeled round.

"You!" snapped Mr Nerdon. "Don't you mess with me!"

"It wasn't *me*!" said Henry. "It was Ralph."

"Liar!" said Mr Nerdon. "Sit at the back of the class."

Horrid Henry moved his seat next to Clever Clare.

"Move over, Henry!" hissed Clare. "You're on my side of the desk."

Henry shoved her.

"Move over yourself," he hissed back.

Then Horrid Henry reached over and broke Clare's pencil.

"Henry broke my pencil!" shrieked Clare.

Mr Nerdon moved Henry next to Weepy William.

Henry pinched him.

Mr Nerdon moved Henry next to Tough Toby.

Henry jiggled the desk.

Mr Nerdon moved Henry next to Lazy Linda.

Henry scribbled all over her paper.

Mr Nerdon moved Henry next to Moody Margaret.

Moody Margaret drew a line down the middle of the desk.

"Cross that line, Henry, and you're dead," said Margaret under her breath.

Henry looked up. Mr Nerdon was writing spelling words on the board.

Henry started to rub out Margaret's line.

"Stop it, Henry," said Mr Nerdon, without turning round.

Henry stopped.

Mr Nerdon continued writing.

Henry pulled Margaret's hair.

Mr Nerdon moved Henry next to Beefy Bert, the biggest boy in the class.

Beefy Bert was chewing his pencil and trying to add 2 + 2 without much luck.

Horrid Henry inched his chair on to Beefy Bert's side of the desk.

Bert ignored him.

Henry poked him.

Bert ignored him.

Henry hit him.

POW!

The next thing Henry knew he was lying on the floor, looking up at the ceiling. Beefy Bert continued chewing his pencil.

"What happened, Bert?" said Mr Nerdon.

"I dunno," said Beefy Bert.

"Get up off the floor, Henry!" said Mr Nerdon. A faint smile appeared on the teacher's slimy lips.

"He hit me!" said Henry. He'd never

felt such a punch in his life.

"It was an accident," said Mr Nerdon. He smirked. "You'll sit next to Bert from now on."

That's it, thought Henry. Now it's war.

"How absurd, to be a nerdy bird," said Horrid Henry behind Mr Nerdon's back.

Slowly Mr Nerdon turned and walked towards him. His hand was clenched into a fist.

"Since you're so good at rhyming," said Mr Nerdon, "everyone write a poem. Now."

Henry slumped in his seat and groaned. A poem! Yuck! He hated poems. Even the word *poem* made him want to throw up.

Horrid Henry caught Rude Ralph's eye. Ralph was grinning and mouthing, "A pound, a pound!" at him. Time was running out. Despite Henry's best efforts, Mr Nerdon still hadn't run screaming from the class. Henry would have to act fast to get that football.

What horrible poem could he write? Horrid Henry smiled. Quickly he picked up his pencil and went to work.

"Now, who's my first victim?" said Mr Nerdon. He looked round the room. "Susan! Read your poem."

Sour Susan stood up and read:

"Bow wow
Bow wow
Woof woof woof
I'm a dog, not a cat, so . . .
SCAT!"

"Not enough rhymes," said Mr

Nerdon. "Next . . ." He looked round
the room. "Graham!"

Greedy Graham stood up and read:

"Chocolate chocolate chocolate sweet,
Cakes and doughnuts can't be beat.
Ice cream is my favourite treat
With lots and lots of pie to eat!"

"Too many rhymes," said Mr Nerdon.
"Next . . ." He scowled at the class.
Henry tried to look as if he didn't want
the teacher to call on him.

"Henry!" snapped Mr Nerdon. "Read
your poem!"

Horrid Henry stood up and read:

"Pirates puke on stormy seas,
Giants spew on top of trees."

Henry peeked at Mr Nerdon. He
looked pale. Henry continued to read:

"Kings are sick in golden loos,
Dogs throw up on Daddy's shoes."

Henry peeked again at Mr Nerdon. He
looked green. Any minute now, thought
Henry, and he'll be out of here
screaming. He read on:

"Babies love to make a mess,
Down the front of Mum's best dress.

87

And what car ride would be complete,
Without the stink of last night's treat?"

"That's enough," choked Mr Nerdon.

"Wait, I haven't got to the good bit," said Horrid Henry.

"I said that's enough!" gasped Mr Nerdon. "You fail."

He made a big black mark in his book.

"I threw up on the boat!" shouted Greedy Graham.

"I threw up on the plane!" shouted Sour Susan.

"I threw up in the car!" shouted Dizzy Dave.

"I said that's enough!" ordered Mr Nerdon. He glared at Horrid Henry. "Get out of here, all of you! It's lunchtime."

Rats, thought Henry. Mr Nerdon was one tough teacher.

Rude Ralph grabbed him.

"Ha ha, Henry," said Ralph. "You lose. Gimme that pound."

"No," said Henry. "I've got until the end of lunch."

"You can't do anything to him between now and then," said Ralph.

"Oh yeah?" said Henry. "Just watch me."

Then Henry had a wonderful, spectacular idea. This was it. The best plan he'd ever had. Someday someone would stick a plaque on the school wall celebrating Henry's genius. There would be songs written about him. He'd probably even get a medal. But first things first. In order for his plan to work to perfection, he needed Peter.

Perfect Peter was playing hopscotch with his friends Tidy Ted and Spotless Sam.

"Hey Peter," said Henry. "How would you like to be a real member of the Purple Hand?"

The Purple Hand was Horrid Henry's secret club. Peter had wanted to join for ages, but naturally Henry would never let him.

Peter's jaw dropped open.

"Me?" said Peter.

"Yes," said Henry. "If you can pass the secret club test."

"What do I have to do?" said Peter eagerly.

"It's tricky," said Henry. "And probably much too hard for you."

"Tell me, tell me," said Peter.

"All you have to do is lie down right there below that window and stay absolutely still. You mustn't move until I tell you to."

"Why?" said Peter.

"Because that's the test," said Henry.

Perfect Peter thought for a moment.

"Are you going to drop something on me?"

"No," said Henry.

"OK," said Peter. He lay down obediently.

"And I need your shoes," said Henry.

"Why?" said Peter.

Henry scowled.

"Do you want to be in the Purple Hand or not?" said Henry.

"I do," said Peter.

"Then give me your shoes and be quiet," said Henry. "I'll be checking on you. If I see you moving one little bit you can't be in my club."

Peter gave Henry his trainers, then lay still as a statue.

Horrid Henry grabbed the shoes, then dashed up the stairs to his classroom.

It was empty. Good.

Horrid Henry went over to the window and opened it. Then he stood there, holding one of Peter's shoes in each hand.

Henry waited until he heard Mr Nerdon's footsteps. Then he went into action.

"Help!" shouted Horrid Henry. "Help!"

Mr Nerdon entered. He saw Henry and glowered.

"What are you doing here? Get out!"

"Help!" shouted Henry. "I can't hold on to him much longer . . . he's slipping . . . aaahhh, he's fallen!"

Horrid Henry held up the empty shoes.

"He's gone," whispered Henry. He peeked out of the window. "Ugghh, I can't look."

Mr Nerdon went pale. He ran to the window and saw Perfect Peter lying still and shoeless on the ground below.

"Oh no," gasped Mr Nerdon.

"I'm sorry," panted Henry. "I tried to hold on to him, honest, I – "

"Help!" screamed Mr Nerdon. He raced down the stairs. "Police! Fire! Ambulance! Help! Help!"

He ran over to Peter and knelt by his still body.

"Can I get up now, Henry?" said Perfect Peter.

"What!?" gasped Mr Nerdon. "What did you say?"

Then the terrible truth dawned. He, Ninius Nerdon, had been tricked.

"YOU HORRID BOY! GO STRAIGHT TO THE HEAD TEACHER – NOW!" screeched Mr Nerdon.

Perfect Peter jumped to his feet.

"But . . . but –" spluttered Perfect Peter.

"Now!" screamed Mr Nerdon. "How dare you! To the head!"

"AAAGGGHHHH," shrieked Peter.

He slunk off to the head's office, weeping.

Mr Nerdon turned to race up the stairs to grab Henry.

"I'll get you, Henry!" he screamed. His face was white. He looked as if he were going to faint.

"Help," squeaked Mr Nerdon.

Then he fainted.

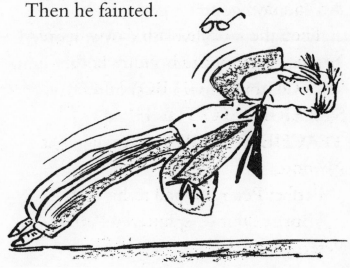

Clunk! Thunk! Thud!

NEE NAW NEE NAW NEE NAW.

When the ambulance arrived, the only person lying on the ground was Mr Nerdon. They scooped him on to a stretcher and took him away.

The perfect end to a perfect day, thought Horrid Henry, throwing his new football in the air. Peter sent home in disgrace. Mr Nerdon gone for good. Even the news that scary Miss Battle-Axe would be teaching Henry's class didn't bother him. After all, tomorrow was another day.